baby animal tales

Goodnight, Little Llama

This book belongs to:

MAGIC CAT PUBLISHING

Once upon a bedtime,
there was a little llama.

She lived with her herd,
high up in the windy mountains.

She had soft brown fur, big brown eyes and long legs
that were just right for skipping and jumping.

Little Llama loved to play with the others,
bouncing through the long mountain grass.

Skip, skip, skippity-skip!

But she was the smallest of the herd
and sometimes she had trouble keeping up.

One day, the llamas decided to climb
to the very top of the windy mountain.

"Up there we'll find the sweetest grass," they said.

Hop, skip, jump!

"Wait for me!" she cried, but the bigger llamas had the wind in their ears and couldn't hear her.

Little Llama was sad. She really wanted to climb the mountain, but she knew she shouldn't do it on her own.

But just then...

Hop!

A small, grey, furry creature
jumped up onto the rock beside her.

"I could climb the mountain with you," he said.
It was her friend, Chinchilla.

He had soft grey fur, big black eyes and strong back
legs just right for hopping and jumping.

Little Llama looked nervously at the chinchilla. "We are so different," she said. "Could we really climb the mountain together?"

"I might look different," said Chinchilla, "but in lots of ways we are the same."

"I love hopping and jumping..." he said.

Hop, skip, jump!

"I like eating the sweet
mountain grass..." he added.

Nibble, nibble, nibble!

"And most of all, I love to climb!
Let me show you the way up the
mountain," he said.

"Will you wait for me if I fall behind?" asked Little Llama.

Chinchilla gave a cheeky chuckle.
"Of course," he said. "That's what friends are for!"

So off they set, up towards the sweetest grass at
the very top of the mountain.

Skip, skippety-skip!
went Little Llama.

Hop, hoppity-hop!
went Chinchilla beside her.

Together they climbed up the whole mountainside and not once did either of them get left behind.

And when they reached the top, they feasted together on the sweet grass until the sun started to slide beneath the clouds and it was time to go home.

On the way down the mountain, Chinchilla started to feel tired and his hops got shorter and shorter and slower and slower.

It was a big mountain to climb for such a small creature.

"Why don't you ride on my back?"
said Little Llama.

"Would that be alright?"
asked Chinchilla hopefully.

"Of course," said Little Llama.
"That's what friends are for."

So Chinchilla hopped up and snuggled down into Little Llama's soft brown fur and was soon fast asleep.

Skip, skippety-skip went Little Llama down, down the mountain, all the way back to the bottom, where her daddy was waiting.

"Chinchilla showed me all the way up!" said Little Llama.

"And Little Llama carried me all the way down!" said Chinchilla.

"That's what friends are for," said Daddy. "And now it's time for bed for both of you."

I wonder what the two friends will do
tomorrow, don't you?

Goodnight, Little Llama!

MAGIC CAT PUBLISHING

Baby Animal Tales © 2020 Magic Cat Publishing Ltd
Text © 2020 Amanda Wood
Photographic illustrations © 2020 Bec Winnel
Photographic images used under license from Shutterstock.com
Illustrations © 2020 Vikki Chu
First Published in 2020 by Magic Cat Publishing Ltd
The Milking Parlour, Old Dungate Farm, Plaistow Road, Dunsfold, Surrey GU8 4PJ, UK

A catalogue record for this book is available from the British Library.

ISBN 978-1-913520-02-1

The illustrations were created digitally
Set in Above the Sky, Recoleta and Cabin

Published by Rachel Williams and Jenny Broom
Designed by Nicola Price

Manufactured in China, TLF0620

9 8 7 6 5 4 3 2 1